The Magic Rabbit

HATS Men's PANTS
Ladies'

PIZZA + SUBS

The Magic Rabbit

Annette Le Blanc Cate

CANDLEWICK PRESS
CAMBRIDGE, MASSACHUSETTS

First edition 2007

Library of Congress Cataloging-in-Publication Data is available.

Library of Congress Catalog Card Number pending

ISBN 978-0-7636-2672-3

2 4 6 8 10 9 7 5 3 1

Printed in China

The text was hand-lettered by the author-illustrator.
The illustrations were done in pen and ink and watercolor.

Candlewick Press
2067 Massachusetts Avenue
Cambridge, Massachusetts 02140

visit us at www.candlewick.com

For Mom and Dad

THE MAGIC OF EGYPT

THE Amazing Ray

Ray and Bunny lived together in a tiny apartment in the city. They were business partners. Ray was a magician, and Bunny was his loyal assistant.

STUFF FOR SHOW

They were also best friends. They did everything together.

Every Saturday, Ray and Bunny took their magic show downtown. But one Saturday, the sidewalk was a little more crowded than usual. And just as Ray said the magic word and Bunny was about to leap from the hat in a spray of glittering stars—

The scene became a terrible tangle of balls and stars, juggler and magician, hat and—
"Bunny? Bunny, where are you?" shouted Ray.
The hat was empty. Bunny was gone!

Meanwhile, the juggler's yipping pug was chasing Bunny down the sidewalk and right into the busy street!

Car horns blared. Bicycle bells rang.

People shouted at the bunny dodging in and out of traffic.

At last, Bunny made it across. He was safe now.

But where was Ray? All Bunny could see were legs and feet. Maybe if Bunny followed them, they would lead him back to Ray.

The feet led him to a beautiful, cool green park. It was a wonderful place for a little bunny, full of squirrels to frolic with and little bits of pretzel to nibble on. But no Ray.

As the sunlight faded away, so did everyone else. Bunny was all alone.

Bunny wandered along the dark street, thinking of Ray and wishing that they were sitting down to dinner together right now, at their own little table in the kitchen.

All around him, people were hurrying home to their own dinners. No one stopped or even seemed to notice the lost little bunny.

Bunny hopped along a little farther, then slipped down a dark alley to rest. He was tired and hungry and missed Ray terribly. A tear rolled down his nose. His nose twitched. Then... his nose twitched again. Bunny smelled something good to eat.

It was popcorn, his favorite!
    Bunny got right to business. As he was nibbling, he noticed something shining among the kernels. Glittering stars! Lots of them!

Bunny followed the path
of stars out of the alley,

along the street...

up a hill...

down some stairs...

and through the subway station, all the way to…

his very own hat!

The last train of the night pulled away.
Only a magician and his bunny assistant were left on the platform.
But two old friends never mind walking home together.